My Aunt Manya

Also by José Patterson

No Buts, Becky!

My Aunt Manya

Based on a true story

by José Patterson

Illustrated by Patricia Drew

Matador
9 Priory Business Park,
Wistow Road, Kibworth Beauchamp,
Leicestershire. LE8 0RX
Tel: 0116 279 2299
Email: books@troubador.co.uk
Web: www.troubador.co.uk/matador
Twitter: @matadorbooks

ISBN 978 1785890 321 (paperback)
ISBN 978 1784625 269 (hardback)

British Library Cataloguing in Publication Data.
A catalogue record for this book is available from the British Library.

Printed and bound in the UK by TJ International, Padstow, UK
Typeset in 12pt Aldine401 BT by Troubador Publishing Ltd, Leicester, UK

Matador is an imprint of Troubador Publishing Ltd

For my good friend Susan Whyman who told me all about Sarah,
her brave grandmother

Acknowledgements

I am indebted to my special friend Jackie Finlay, without whose unflagging help *My Aunt Manya* would not have been published and to Patricia Drew for her wonderful illustrations.

Chapter 1

Sarah looked round quickly to make sure Leah, her stepmother, couldn't hear.

"It's no use looking at me like that, Vaska," she whispered to her black cat purring loudly beside her. He sat perfectly still, his all-seeing green eyes fixed steadily on her face.

"The thing is, Vaska, Papa can't save the fish heads for you because he's not here. He's gone to look for a job on the other side of the world. Look Vaska, I'll prove it to you." The cat watched her closely as she scrabbled about in her pocket. "Here it is," she said, flourishing a crumpled letter. "See, it's from America and addressed to me here in Piliki in Russia and the postmark is dated September 1891. Papa's in New York living with his sister, my Aunt Manya." She played with one of her long brown plaits and frowned. "It's not fair, Vaska. He should have taken me with him. I'm not a baby you know. I'm nearly eleven years old. Aunt Manya wouldn't mind and I'm sure she wouldn't order me about like SHE does. I hate being left behind with HER," she stopped for a moment to watch the cat's twitching tail. "I can never do anything right and SHE criticises me all the time and makes me do some of the rough work in the kitchen. That's supposed to be Olga's job, not mine. I'll tell you something else, Vaska. I feel sorry for Olga. SHE gives her orders in Yiddish which we speak, but Olga only speaks Russian. No wonder the poor girl gets muddled. I don't know about you Vaska, but it seems to me that Olga and I are always in some kind of trouble with HER. SHE doesn't love me like Mama, God rest her soul, did."

Sarah looked up to see Yanek the postman wave as he walked past the house. "No letter from Papa again," she sighed. "I'm sick and tired of telling myself that his letters take a long time to get here." She swallowed hard and screwed up her eyes, but even that couldn't stop hot tears trickling down her cheeks and dripping slowly on to the cat. As if to comfort her, Vaska stretched himself, nudged her chin with the top of his head and curled up in her lap.

She was suddenly startled by the sound of familiar footsteps. They were quick and heavy – a sure sign that trouble was on its way. Vaska heard them too. He leapt off Sarah's lap and fled like a streak of lightning.

"Olga's gone!" Leah shouted angrily, gasping to get her breath back. "I've sent her packing. Stupid, careless, clumsy peasant girl. Come and see what she's done!" She pointed to a storage jar which lay smashed to pieces scattering yeast all over the floor.

2

"See, d'you see," she snorted. "I can't start baking *challah* bread for *Shabbos* without yeast."

Sarah bit her lip as she looked down at the mess. *The smell of yeast always makes me think of Mama when I used to help bake the challahs. It was my job to sprinkle poppy seeds over them before they went in the oven.*

"Here," Leah snapped. "Take this money and get me some from the baker. Don't dawdle. Be quick about it."

As soon as Sarah was out of the house she bumped into Yanek. "I'm glad I've seen you, Sarah. I walked right past your house earlier and forgot this." He handed her a package and hurried on.

She turned her precious parcel over and over. *It's from Papa! At last! Shall I open it now?* she asked herself. *Is it good news or bad news? Has Papa got a job or is he still looking? Does he like living in New York with Aunt Manya? I hope he's missing me,* she sighed as she put the parcel safely in her pocket. "I'll open it later so I have something to look forward to," she murmured.

The baker's shop was heaven on earth! Sarah's nostrils quivered with the warm, comforting, yeasty smell of freshly baked breads, delicious cakes and pastries piled high on the counter and on shelves around the shop. What a choice! Black bread, bagels, rye bread, plaited challahs, crusty rolls, onion rolls, apple strudel, sponge cakes, cheesecakes – the list was a long one.

The baker gave Sarah the packet of yeast then stopped. "Just a minute! Aren't you Joseph and Malka's little friend, Sarah?"

Sarah nodded.

"'Course you are, and that's good because I've just remembered something. Wait there." He rummaged under the counter.

"Malka was in the shop earlier and left this behind," he said, holding out a bag of bagels. "She's always in a hurry, that woman! Can you take them to her? It'll be a shame to let them go stale."

Sarah nodded again.

"Good girl. I knew you would. And this is for you," he smiled as he handed her a slice of caraway seed cake.

She had just reached the door when he called out. "Sarah, come back here, I've got something else for you." She munched happily on her cake while she watched him scribble a note and fold it up. "Give this to Joseph, it's important," he said quietly.

Sarah hadn't gone far before the tantalising smell of fresh baked bagels – a roll with a hole, she used to call them when she was little – was just too tempting. She grabbed one and took a first delicious crispy bite.

"I know Malka won't mind," she spluttered with her mouth full. "She's generous and kind and so is Joseph. Between the two of them they've looked after me like a second mother. I'll open my parcel with them. They'll be just as excited as I am." Malka answered the knock on her door and couldn't help smiling when she saw Sarah, crumbs round her mouth, clutching a parcel and a bag of bagels.

"Come in, child. What a kind girl you are to bring my bagels." She pretended to count them. "I hope you were hungry enough to eat one or two on the way here!" she laughed and winked at her. "Joseph," she called out, "my special bagel messenger has just arrived!"

"Look, look, I've got a parcel from Papa!" she shouted. "I don't know what's in it. Oh yes, and this is for you, Joseph," she said, handing him the note from the baker.

"There's only one way to find out, Sarah," Joseph smiled, pocketing the note. "Calm down child, and open it."

Sarah could feel the pulse in her throat and her hands began to tremble as she started to unwrap the package. Inside was an old book. She let her fingers slide gently over the black leather cover. "I know what it is," she nodded excitedly. "It's Papa's Hebrew daily prayer book. Look! Here's his name on the inside cover. I remember him telling me that as well as all our prayers, Jews have a blessing for almost everything you can think of and this book is full of them!" She smiled as she turned over the pages. "Oh! What's this?" she asked as an envelope slid out from between the pages. "I expect this is for me too." She opened it carefully and found a letter, a ticket and some money. She unfolded the letter, carefully smoothed the creases out and then examined it closely.

"*Oy vey* – bother," she said, frowning hard. "I hate grown-up scribble! I can't make it out at all!" She looked at it again. "It doesn't look much like Papa's writing either. I don't understand. Will you read it please, Joseph?" she asked, tugging on her plaits while she waited. Joseph's head was bent low over the letter so she couldn't see the grave expression on his face.

"Well, are you going to tell me? What's the news?"

"My dear child," Joseph hesitated, then went on: "I'm afraid that it's bad news and …" he stopped and looked at her. Sarah's face was as white as a sheet.

"It's Papa, isn't it? Isn't it? Something terrible has happened to him, hasn't it? Tell me," she whimpered, "please tell me."

Joseph gripped her hands tightly. "Boris, your dear father, God rest his soul, has been killed in a road accident," he said gravely. "This letter is from your Aunt Manya. She wants you to go and live with her in New York. She's sent you a boat ticket and some money for the journey."

Sarah sat quite still as if she were in a trance. "Oh Papa! Papa!" she cried. Then she slowly stroked her cheeks and round her chin – the very places where Papa used to tickle her with his beard. How vividly she remembered reading with him, going for walks with him, sitting next to him on his wagon, and best of all, in his carpenter's workshop, a row of nails pressed carefully between his lips and his hammer gripped firmly in his strong hand. When the memory faded she felt the blood drain from her face and a strange buzzing in her ears as if she were going to faint. It was only when Malka's strong arms were round her that she broke down and sobbed loudly as if her heart would break.

Joseph shook his head sadly. "Malka," he whispered, "take her to our room and let her cry as long as she needs to, poor child. Boris was a *mensch,* a good human being. I must go and break the sad news to Leah, and then go to the Rabbi to ask him to say prayers for him. We must start making plans for Sarah as soon as I get back."

It was dark by the time Joseph returned and Malka had drawn the curtains and lit the two *Shabbos* candles. He looked at Sarah's pale face and her sad eyes, red and puffy from crying. "God help this poor child," he prayed quietly, "heaven alone knows how she'll manage the dangers of the longest journey of her young life."

"I can't go," she announced suddenly.

"What do you mean, you can't go?" Malka sounded shocked. "What are you talking about?"

"SHE won't let me. SHE's just got rid of Olga so she won't spare me."

"Nonsense, child! Your Aunt Manya has a much stronger claim on you than Leah. You've been sent a boat ticket and some money and what's more," she said sternly, "Joseph and I will make sure that you're going to use them. You'll stay here with us until everything is ready for your journey."

"Listen to me," Joseph said quietly, folding Sarah's hands in his. "You're a sensible girl and what I've got to say is very important. The note you gave me from Issy the baker was to warn me that a group of Cossacks – Russian soldiers – are camped in the next village. He got a message from a non-Jewish Russian friend of his. Thank God for friends like that," he sighed. "I don't need to tell you that Cossacks hate us Jews, and can't wait to start a pogrom which as you know, is a cruel, murderous attack on innocent Jewish people," he sighed again. "I know you've hardly had time to take in what's happened but Malka and I need to act quickly to get you out of here. You've got the chance of a lifetime to go to America. You've got to take it."

Just hearing the words 'pogrom' and 'Cossacks' made Sarah stiffen with fear. *I'll never forget listening to Papa telling Mama about a pogrom in a far off town. Cossacks, Russian soldiers, who wore long coats and tall black fur hats shaped like drums, whipped their horses into a frenzy and, waving their sabres, charged into the town trampling on anyone in their path and killing hundreds of innocent Jewish people. Papa had tears in his eyes when he heard that some of his relatives had been killed. He bent his head and his shoulders started to shake. He was sobbing. I'd never seen a man cry before.*

"What will you and Malka do and what will SHE do? *Oy vey* – bother!" Sarah put one hand over her mouth and the other in her pocket and slowly pulled out a squashed packet of yeast.

"Malka's going to look after her old mother who lives in a small village not too far from here. It'll be safer there. I'll join her when I can. We'll come back when it's all quiet again. I warned Leah and she's making plans to stay with her niece until the trouble is over. She was complaining about not being able to bake challahs," he nodded at Sarah and then went on. "You know, Sarah, I can't help thinking that if little Olga hadn't accidentally smashed that pot of yeast this morning things might have turned out differently. It was meant to happen – it's – *Beshert*!"

"What's that?"

"Beshert is the Yiddish word for fate. It was meant to happen."

"Beshert," Sarah repeated. "It was meant to happen."

Before I forget … thank you, Aunt Manya, for sending me Papa's prayer book, a boat ticket and some money. I'm very sad about my dear Papa, but I'm sure I'm going to feel at home with you. You have given me a chance to escape from the Cossacks. They give me nightmares. Tomorrow I'm going to start the same long journey Papa made. I don't know how long it'll take and I'm trying hard not to be afraid. I know you'll be waiting for me and that will keep me going. I'll miss Malka and Joseph and my other friends and Vaska, my black cat, but I won't miss HER.

Chapter 2

It was barely light when they left. Only the crowing of a cockerel broke the still silent morning. Joseph gave an encouraging click with his tongue, tugged on Sivka's reins and the old wagon rumbled out of the yard. Sarah, hunched up against the cold, was deep in thought. *I didn't know it could be so hard saying goodbye to Malka and my friends. Everyone's been so kind – except HER. Malka gave me one of her own cases for my luggage, and Anastasia embroidered a handkerchief for me.* She stroked the lovely warm scarf from Feyga and the knitted mittens from Dina. *And as for Papa's apprentice sweet, shy Sergey,* Sarah smiled to herself, *he actually blushed when he gave me the cake his mother had baked for me. Best of all Katerina, who loves cats as much as I do, has promised to feed Vaska.*

Sarah had no idea how far they travelled that first day. She pestered Joseph with her worries about the Cossacks and pogroms until he almost lost his patience. She was stiff, tired, hungry and every bone in her body was aching when they arrived at Joseph's friends, Yossie and Lila.

She was lifted down from the wagon and carried inside to a warm place next to the crackling logs in the central brick stove, its long chimney stretching up through the roof. "Here you are Sarah," said Lila kindly, handing her a cup of tea and a slice of black bread. "This will keep you going until supper. The men are busy in the stable but as soon as they get back we'll eat." She bent down and kissed the top of Sarah's head. "Your dear father stayed here too when he was on his way to America," she nodded to herself. "I know he would have been very proud of you." She nodded to herself. "Yes, he certainly would," she murmured.

Supper consisted of a dish – a big dish Sarah couldn't help noticing – filled with steaming hot *tzimmes* – a delicious vegetable stew of mainly carrots, raisins and a few small pieces of meat. By the time Sarah had cleared her plate, she could hardly keep her eyes open. Lila had made a bed for her in the far corner of the room.

"Sleep well, child. You'll need all your strength for the long journey ahead of you. God bless."

"Papa was here," Sarah whispered sleepily to herself. "He was here in this very room. I hope he dreamt of me that night. I'll be dreaming of him."

★ ★ ★

A loud commotion in the yard woke Sarah with a start. She dressed quickly and ran outside to find Joseph and Yossie struggling to back Sivka into the wagon shafts.

"A carrot!" Sarah shouted, "she'll do anything for a carrot." She was right – it worked like a charm and the horse was soon harnessed. As soon as Sarah took her seat next to Joseph, Lila gave her a bag of bread and fruit for their journey. She had tears in her eyes when she kissed her goodbye. "Keep in touch when you can, my dear," she whispered. "I've said it before and I'll say it again, your dear Papa would be very proud of you."

Sarah was deep in thought as they travelled along. There were so many questions she wanted to ask Joseph in spite of testing his patience again.

"Where are we going next Joseph? Are we safe now from the Cossacks? Are we far enough away from them? What …" She didn't finish her last question because she was watching Sivka tossing her head up and down. Suddenly the horse stumbled heavily on some slippery cobblestones, lost her footing and slithered to the ground. The wagon tipped sideways and they all landed in a ditch!

Sarah groaned, then winced in pain as she rubbed her neck and shoulder. She looked down at her torn skirt spattered with lumps of mud and grass.

"STUPID, STUPID, HORSE!" she shouted at the top of her voice. "Why couldn't you look where you were going? You might have killed us both. The wagon's broken and we can't move on and we're stuck here and the Cossacks will catch us up and kill us and … and I'll … I'll never get to see my Aunt Manya," she sobbed.

Joseph picked her up in his arms and carried her to a patch of clean grass.

"Calm down child and don't upset yourself. Don't blame the horse. These quiet roads are very old and always in need of repair. Sit here and rest. I've got some work to do." He untangled the bridle and the reins and lifted the shafts away from the horse so he could tether her to a tree trunk. He stood looking down at the wagon. It was all too clear that he couldn't pull it out of the ditch single-handedly.

Meanwhile Sarah was busy picking bits of grass and twigs out of her hair. "I'm sorry I lost my temper, Joseph," she sniffed as she wiped her nose on her sleeve. She looked up, then stood up, then started to jump and wave her arms about until she was breathless.

"Joseph, look, look! Can you see what's coming?" she gasped.

Travelling towards them from the opposite direction was a farmer driving his horse and cart loaded with vegetables.

It didn't take long for the two strong men working together – with grunts and groans – to pull the wagon out of the ditch and make a good job of fixing one of the bent shafts. The farmer not only refused to take any money for his trouble, but made sure that Sarah and Joseph were well supplied with potatoes, cabbages and a bag of onions thrown in for good measure.

"And now, Sarah, I'll try and answer some of your questions," Joseph said when they were back on the road again. "We're safe from Cossacks on these narrow roads. They stick to the towns. We've got one more stop with Malka's Aunt Eva."

"What's she like?" Sarah asked.

"She's a good cook and makes a delicious potato *kugel*."

"Potato pudding is one of my favourites too. What else?"

"She's, you know, well she's …" Joseph hesitated and scratched his head. "Oh, I don't know, Sarah, you'll have to wait and see for yourself."

And Sarah did see – very clearly! Aunt Eva had twinkling eyes set in her wrinkled face and her thick white hair was scraped back in a bun. She was kind, capable, loved fussing over her relatives and made Sarah gasp for breath when she was greeted with a big hug and squeeze. Sarah soon discovered that Aunt Eva did not believe in cutting corners. Not only did she mend and wash Sarah's skirt, but everything she stood up in, from top to bottom!

"Come here, child," she said, wrapping her in a blanket and leading her to a cosy spot near the big wood stove. "Sit here and dry your hair, then I'll plait it for you. The water in the samovar kettle is boiling so I'll make you a cup of tea and slice some bread while we're waiting for Joseph. Are you hungry?" she asked.

"I'm starving," Sarah laughed, "and the smell of the *kugel* is making my mouth water."

"Good! That's what I like to hear." Just then Joseph came in from the yard. "Good," she repeated. "It's time for supper."

The potato pudding was delicious, there was plenty of it, and there wasn't a scrap wasted!

Aunt Eva smiled. "I don't mind telling you that if it wasn't for the potatoes and onions you brought, your supper would have been a bowl of bean soup and bread and herrings."

"I know what you're going to say!" Sarah giggled. "It was meant to happen – it's *beshert*!"

13

Before I forget … I wonder if Papa told you what I look like, Aunt Manya? In case he didn't I've got two long dark brown plaits which I'm always fidgeting with, greyish blue eyes, and a nose that goes sideways. Mama used to say that one day I would be a beautiful girl. I'm nearly grown up but it hasn't happened yet. I think I'll just have to keep waiting.

Chapter 3

"Whoa!" With much creaking and groaning, the wagon rumbled to a halt.

"We're getting close now, Sarah," Joseph said quietly.

"What are we going to do?"

"We have to stay here until it's dark and wait for a signal from my good friend Ivan. He'll take you through the forest to the place where the guide will be waiting to smuggle you and lots of other people across the border. The border guards are always on the lookout for anyone trying to get from one country into another without a passport, without official papers. Don't worry, child," he said looking at Sarah's anxious face, "Ivan will look after you. He knows the way through the forest like the back of his hand."

Sarah shivered and pulled her shawl tightly round her shoulders. "If they catch me, they'll send me back to Piliki and back to HER," Sarah whispered hoarsely, trying hard not to cry.

"Shame on you, Sarah Nossovsky, what kind of talk is that?" Joseph muttered as he put his arm round her shoulders. "Listen to me, child. I helped your father, God rest his soul, and he got safely over the border into Germany, didn't he? Then he got a train to the port in Bremerhaven, and then a boat to America, didn't he? Well, answer me, didn't he?"

"Yes, he did," Sarah sniffed. "I ..." she choked, then swallowed, "I ... I ... just can't believe I'll never see him again," she mumbled through her tears.

Joseph pulled her closer. "It was a shock for Malka and me as well. But you're a lucky girl, you know. You've got a very kind aunt waiting to give you a good home. You'll have a new life in a free country where you'll be safe from the fear of pogroms."

"But I ..."

Joseph raised his hand. "I'm not listening to any more of your arguments. Everything's been planned very carefully. Ivan will help you, I promise."

Sarah looked up. The purple dome of the sky was streaked with the last thin shafts of light. The silence was broken suddenly by a flock of wild geese outlined against the darkening skyline, honking noisily, in a perfect 'V' formation as they flew past. She watched them until they vanished over the horizon. *If only I could fly over the border just like them*, she thought wistfully. Sivka tossed her head and snorted. A swirling mist rose up from the river, curled around the wagon then disappeared into thin air.

"Look over there Joseph!" Sarah hissed, tugging at his sleeve. "Did you see that? No? I'm sure I saw something. I think it was a sort of twinkling light." They sat bolt upright straining their eyes on the distant dark horizon. Nothing happened. *Perhaps I'm dreaming,* Sarah thought. *I'm sure Joseph thinks I'm being childish and just imagining things. Please, please let something happen soon. I'm sick and tired of all this watching and waiting.* Suddenly she saw a small light flashing in the blackness.

"A light!" Sarah pointed. "I'm sure of it now. There it is again." This time there was no mistaking it. Just below the line of the distant pine trees they saw a flickering light – on, then off, on, then off. It was the signal they were waiting for! "Good. Let's go." Joseph said, gathering up the horse's reins.

"Have you hidden your money and your ticket?"

Sarah patted the bulge – the precious cotton bag which Malka had made for her and stitched inside her petticoat. "It's quite safe here. I even managed to save it from Aunt Eva. It's the one single thing she didn't get to wash!"

"Don't let anyone see you feeling for it. There are too many thieves out there – even Jewish ones! But you can trust Ivan. Lie still now and keep as quiet as a mouse. God bless you child," Joseph whispered as he kissed the top of her head. Then he gently pushed her down in the wagon and covered her with straw.

Sarah heard him crack his whip and urge the horse on. With a sudden jolt the wagon lurched forward bumping along the uneven cart track. She could see the stars twinkling above her through the layers of stale, sour-smelling straw. It scratched her skin and poked up her nose. She had to tense every muscle in her body to stop herself from sneezing. In spite of Joseph's kindness, she couldn't help feeling scared at the words 'smugglers' and 'frontier' and 'border guards'. *Will we be stopped at the border town between Poland and Germany? Supposing I'm caught and they arrest Papa's friends and send me back to HER?* Sarah thought with a shudder. *Please God,* she prayed, *don't let them catch me. Not now, not after coming so far.*

Before I forget … I think you ought to know, Aunt Manya, that I'm very good at worrying! Papa used to tease me about it. "You could worry the hind leg off a donkey!" he would laugh. Just the same I think that anyone who is about to go through a big forest for the first time is bound to get the shivers, don't you? I've already got a strange feeling in the pit of my stomach. Does that count as worry?

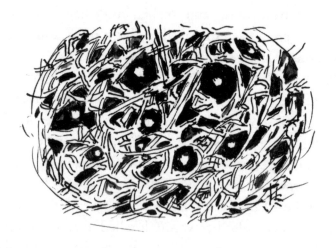

Chapter 4

"Stop!" The voice sounded gruff and agitated. "Where's the girl?" Sarah felt her body stiffen with fear as the wagon jolted to a standstill. She was so scared she could hardly breathe. *Who is that man – is he a friend or an enemy? Is it one of the guards searching for illegal immigrants? Has Joseph driven me to the wrong place? What's happened to Ivan? Please, please don't let them find me. Don't let them hand me over to the guards*, she prayed under her breath, pressing her body further down in the straw. Suddenly she felt a shaft of cold air as the straw was brushed aside and two strong arms lifted her to the ground.

"Who are you?" she asked. "Are you Ivan?"

A large hand was pressed gently over her mouth.

"Yes," he said, removing his hand and gripping hers, "but from now on there's to be no talking. Do you hear me? Come, we must go."

Sarah wrenched her hand free and ran back to give Joseph one last hug and kiss. "Thank you and Malka for everything," she gulped, brushing away her tears. "Don't forget to save some fish heads for Vaska."

She took Ivan's hand again and they set off through the forest guided only by the light of a pale watery moon. The only sounds which broke the silence were owls hooting, leaves rustling, twigs snapping under their feet and the forest wildlife scurrying for the safety of the dark undergrowth. It was cold and damp in the forest, but Sarah was glad enough to breathe in the smell of scented pine trees after the stifling air in the wagon.

Papa must have walked this very same path with Ivan. Was he as scared as I am? she wondered. There were so many questions she wanted to ask Ivan about her father, but she daren't – not now. Nothing else mattered except trying to keep up with him. She half ran, stumbling again and again over fallen branches and half buried roots of trees which littered the path. When she fell and scratched her face she had to bite her tongue to stop herself crying out in pain. Ivan stopped only long enough to pick her up, pat her on the head, grip her hand and set off again. She had no idea how long they had been going when suddenly she heard a deafening blast of gunfire.

"They're shooting at us, they're going to kill us!" Sarah gasped. She drew in her breath ready to scream. Ivan, who was watching her closely, was too quick for her. He covered her mouth again – and this time it was anything but gentle. When he took his hand away from her face her whole body was

shaking with shock. She could feel her heart thumping hard in her ribcage, and as the blood drained from her face she dropped to the ground on her knees.

Ivan gripped her shoulders in his strong hands and helped her to her feet.

"Listen to me child," he whispered. "As long as the soldiers are busy shooting at other smugglers, they won't bother us. We can't stop here, it's too dangerous." He shook his head. "It's too dangerous," he said again. "We've got to keep going. Do you understand? We've got no choice." He grabbed her hand. "Come!"

The sound of firing bullets died away. *The shooting has stopped but where are the guards now?* Sarah asked herself. *Are they moving closer? Are they reloading their rifles?* Every twig that snapped, every leaf that rustled, anything that scurried across their path, in fact any strange sound made Sarah twitch and jump and stiffen with fright until Ivan was half carrying her as they hurried along. Then everything happened at once. They heard loud voices coming nearer and without warning bullets began to whistle over their heads.

"Don't scream!" Ivan hissed, his hand ready to cover Sarah's mouth. "Look, the moon's just gone behind the clouds. They can't see us. Keep close behind me!" She ran after him as fast as she could, her mind racing. *Keep going, Sarah. Don't listen for shots. Don't think about being frightened. Don't think about your aches and pains. Keep going because if you don't, not only your life but Ivan's will be in danger.* She was right behind him as he moved forward crouching in and out of low lying shrubs and the thick shelter of leafy branches. He stopped suddenly and stood quite still, listening intently. Then, at the very second when the moon slipped out from behind the clouds, a salvo of bullets whistled past their heads and landed with a sickening thud behind them. *They know where we are. They can see us! They're going to kill us!* Before she knew what was happening Ivan had pulled her down into a ditch and covered them with overhanging branches and greenery. Sarah clung to him and buried her face in his thick cloth coat which smelled of damp earth. It was impossible to know how long they sat in the ditch straining to listen for sounds of shooting. Sarah was numb with cold and her limbs were stiff when, with a quiet nudge, Ivan pulled her out. He rubbed her hands quickly to get her circulation going again so they could move on. On and on they went in silence until at long last the great canopy of trees began to thin out as they came to a clearing at the edge of the forest.

"This is as far as I can go," Ivan told her. "Can you see that shed down there?" he said, pointing to the bottom of a slope. "Yes? Go in there and wait for the guide. He knows the area very well and he'll take you and the others to safety. Here, give him this," he said, pushing some money into her hand.

"Thank you," she gulped wiping the tears from her face.

"You're a very brave girl, Sarah. Your father, God rest his soul, was a real mensch. He would be very proud of you," he muttered, pressing her to him before quickly disappearing back into the forest.

Sarah flopped down under the shelter of a thick leafy bush, wrapped her skirt round her knees, closed her eyes and breathed in deeply. Her throat tightened and she swallowed hard to stop herself from crying. "Ivan risked his life for me," she sniffed. "I can't let him down now. I've got to keep going." She stood up, wiped her face, grabbed her bag, pulled her shawl tightly round her shoulders and followed the rough track to the door of a long low building. She pushed it open very slowly and walked into a dark room packed with people standing around murmuring quietly to each other. The air was thick with tobacco smoke and sounds of men inhaling, exhaling and coughing. The only light, apart from one small lantern, seemed to come from the glow of cigarettes which, Sarah thought, looked just like clusters of glow worms. She stood near the door until her eyes adjusted to the semi-darkness. The cold from the damp wall set her teeth chattering. "I know what's wrong with you Sarah Nossovsky," she muttered to herself through clenched teeth, "you're scared again. That's it, isn't it? Go on, admit it." She took a few deep breaths and then she went on: "Grow up Sarah! This place is packed with people you've never seen before in your life. Strangers, yes, but enemies, no! How could they be? They're here for exactly the same reason as you are – running away from a pogrom and trying to cross the border. I'm sure there's no one here who would want to harm you." She moved forward slowly, groping along the wall and carefully taking one small step at a time. As she was feeling her way round she tripped over something and landed on the floor with a thud.

"Are you hurt?" A woman with a kind voice whispered gently as she helped her up. "No? Well thank God for that. I think you must have fallen over my big feet. They always seem to get in everyone's way! Who are you with?"

"No one. I'm on my own."

"Alone? How come you're alone?" the voice repeated. "Who are you, child, and how did you get here all by yourself?"

"I'm Sarah Nossovsky and I'm nearly eleven years old. My parents are dead. Papa's friend, Ivan, brought me through the forest. The guards shot at us and I was terrified. We were nearly killed and …" her voice trailed off and ended with a sob.

Sarah felt a strong arm round her shoulders. "I'm Rosa Kaplansky and I'm travelling on my own too and I think it'll be a good idea if we stick together, don't you? Yes? Come with me, child."

Rosa led her to a door at the back of the shed. There was just enough moonlight in the yard for Sarah to see a well and a bucket of water next to it.

"You thirsty?" Rosa asked and without waiting for an answer, dipped a tin cup into the bucket and gave it to Sarah.

"That's better, eh?" she smiled as Sarah drained the cup and wiped her mouth with the back of her hand.

"One more thing." She dipped a piece of rag in the water and carefully bathed Sarah's scratches, wiped the mud from her face and picked out the leaves and twigs in her hair.

"There now. That's the best I can do in this light. You poor child. I hate to think what you must have gone through in the forest. You must be exhausted and I'm sure you could do with a good rest, but I'm afraid that's not possible." She shook her head and sighed. "As soon as the guide turns up we'll be on our way. In the meantime take this," she said, offering Sarah a piece of black bread and cheese.

"Thanks, I'm starving," she mumbled with her mouth full.

Rosa was right. There was no time to rest. The guide arrived, collected money from everyone and gave strict orders to walk silently in single file behind him.

"That rule doesn't apply to you and me, child," Rosa muttered quietly as she gripped Sarah's hand. There was a strong wind blowing hard in their faces as they set off.

The moon slipped in and out from behind dark clouds making it difficult to see the path ahead. *Come on, Sarah, keep going, keep going*, she told herself over and over again, wincing with the pain of the stitch in her side. *If only we could stop and rest so I can get my breath back*, she thought, as they trudged along. At long last they stopped at a shallow part of a river. The guide whispered instructions to remove their boots. Sarah tied her boot laces together and hung them round her neck then put one foot in the water. She sucked in her breath ready to scream when Rosa quickly covered her mouth.

"Don't scream!" she hissed, dropping her hand. "The water's freezing, I know, but you'll get used to it."

"It's so co … co … cold," Sarah stuttered through chattering teeth.

"Courage, Sarah. I'll rub your feet when we get to the other side."

Numbed with cold and clinging on to Rosa, she hitched up her skirt and waded across the icy water. It was tough going. She slithered and squelched in the deep mud and thick weeds which grew on the river bed. She had to bite her tongue to stop herself from crying out in pain when she trod on sharp stones and gravel. From the sounds of the muffled groans and moans around her she wasn't the only one!

"Brave girl!" Rosa murmured, pulling her up on to the bank and massaging her frozen, bleeding feet.

"Please God," she prayed under her breath. "Give me strength to keep up with everyone else. And thank you for Rosa," she said quietly. Half walking and half stumbling, Sarah forced herself on and on.

"We're nearly there, Sarah, I'm sure of it. This guide is very skilful. You see where he's taking us now, making sure that we all keep close to small woods and copses where we can hide quickly if we're in danger. Rest assured, he's done this many times before!"

At long last they stopped at the top of a wooded hill. The first streaks of dawn were slowly lighting up the morning sky in a pale pink glow. Below them they could just see the faint outlines of houses, churches, and the black ribbons of railway tracks. Sarah could feel her heart hammering with excitement. In spite of feeling exhausted, she wanted to run down the hill shouting at the top of her voice!

"Is this …?"

"Yes, yes – THIS IS IT! The border town of Eydtkuhnen!" Rosa interrupted, grabbing hold of Sarah and showering her with hugs and kisses. "We've made it!" she laughed. "Now, what d'you say to a cup of tea and a cake as soon as the first baker's shop opens? After that our next stop will be the port of Bremerhaven!"

"Rosa," Sarah asked shyly. "Can I tell you something?"

"Of course you can. What's the matter?"

"Well, I keep thinking about that hut. It was packed full of strangers and I didn't know anybody – not one single person. I'm so lucky that it was your feet I tripped over. It's beshert isn't it? It was meant to happen."

Rosa looked as if she was going to cry.

"Well, isn't it?" Sarah asked again.

Rosa nodded and kissed her again. Her cheeks were wet with tears. "Yes, my dear child," she coughed as if she had difficulty in speaking. Then she smiled. "There's no doubt about it, none at all. It's beshert."

Before I forget … have you ever been really and truly terrified, Aunt Manya? I was in the forest. Everything happens inside your body. First my heart wasn't just beating very fast, it was hammering so hard I was sure Ivan heard it. I couldn't breathe properly, my hands were shaking, my legs trembled all the time and my feet were numb with cold. My new friend, Rosa, told me it's best to forget all about it, and she's right. No one can keep being frightened about being frightened, can they?!

Chapter 5

"That's the Bremerhaven train over there," Rosa shouted. "See it? Hold my hand tightly and whatever happens don't let go." Sarah didn't need telling twice. She clung on to her like a limpet.

There was a deafening roar inside the railway station: belching steam and smoke, piercing whistles and screeching brakes. The platform was packed tight from end to end with worried, exhausted passengers clutching screaming babies and little children, as well as suitcases, boxes, bulging bags and bundles of all shapes and sizes. Everyone was shouting, swearing and pushing as they fought their way on to the waiting train.

"Phew!" Rosa gasped with relief as they sat down. "I

bet you thought we'd never make it, didn't you?" she asked, watching Sarah brush the hair away from her tired face and tie up her plaits. Her eyes were heavy with lack of sleep.

"Poor child, you must be so tired," Rosa murmured gently.

"I've never seen so many people in all my life," Sarah gasped. "I thought we'd be crushed to death in that madhouse! And all that luggage! Did you see that man carrying a samovar! A great big brass samovar kettle of all things!" she giggled. "You're wonderful, Rosa. I don't know how you did it, pulling and pushing me through the crowd like that. I'm sure I would have been trampled underfoot."

"It was more like burrowing!" Rosa tidied some stray hairs back into her thick bun and wiped the sweat off her face with the back of her hand. "It was simple really. We could move quickly because we're both travelling light. My carpet bag isn't very heavy and neither is your flour sack. How on earth did you manage to get hold of that?"

"Papa's kind friends, Malka and Joseph insisted I stay with them just before we left. My stepmother didn't care because she was in a hurry to get away – we all were. We were very frightened the Cossacks were coming to start a pogrom. SHE just had time to give Joseph a few of my clothes in a parcel. Malka gave me one of her own cases but it broke when it fell off Joseph's wagon. We stayed with relatives and friends on our way to the forest and one of them gave me this sack. It's been washed y'know, and it's very strong."

"Your stepmother sounds as if she was a mean sort of woman, so in my opinion, I think you're well rid of her," Rosa said with some feeling.

Sarah didn't answer. She chewed her lip and played with her plaits. "SHE didn't like me, Rosa, in fact I think SHE hated me," she blurted out at last. "SHE was horrible to me when Papa left home. I'm going to New York to live with his sister, my Aunt Manya. I hope she'll love me like Mama did," she murmured, trying to hold back her tears.

"Don't you fret child, because there's no need. I'm quite certain your father said good things about you when he was with your aunt. Besides, she sent you a ticket didn't she?"

Sarah nodded.

"D'you know how much it cost? No? Well I do because my brother sent me one. Twenty five dollars! Did you hear that? Yes? Twenty five dollars," she repeated. She nodded to herself, as if she was trying to work out its true value. "That's a lot of money, Sarah, you'd better believe me. I bet your aunt saved up two dollars every week until she'd paid it off. Now if that isn't proof that she loves you, I don't know what is."

Rosa was right. Just thinking about it made her feel all warm inside, just like the time when Papa once gave her a sip of his vodka. *I wonder what Aunt Manya looks like*, she thought, looking round the packed carriage. The woman by the window was snoring loudly with her mouth wide open. Sarah shook her head. *Not her.* The next one was so fat she blocked Sarah's view! She leant forward and looked at the woman who was squashed in the far corner. She had several chins wobbling gently with the rocking motion of the train. *Definitely not her! Be patient*, she frowned, *you've just got to be patient.* She looked out of the window. The train had gathered speed and was rattling past hills and rivers and forests, animals grazing in fields, and small villages with wooden houses and tall churches.

"I bet travelling from Piliki wasn't as fast as this, was it?" Rosa asked.

Sarah shook her head. "No it wasn't. It was so slow I was scared stiff all the time that the Cossacks would catch us up. Joseph calmed me down. He was good like that," she smiled thoughtfully. "I've no idea how long we bumped along in his creaky old wagon pulled by his stubborn horse Sivka. Wherever we stopped with friends or relations, they shared their food with us. Am I talking too much, Rosa?"

"No you're not. Go on, go on."

"We were always welcomed with a warm seat next to the stove and clean straw and fodder for the horse. I'd never seen any of those people before in my whole life, yet we were treated as if we were members of the family." She looked at Rosa who was nodding and listening. "You've been just as kind to me Rosa."

"No need to thank me. I'm glad to help. There can't be many children like you who are brave enough to go all by themselves to New York. Anyway, I'm on my own too, y'know."

"Rosa can I ask you something?"

"'Course you can. Ask away!" Rosa nodded.

"I don't mean to be rude, but is your husband waiting for you in America?" she asked shyly.

"I'm not married – yet!" Rosa laughed, "But my two sisters are and so is my brother who lives in New York. I looked after my father until he died, so I had no reason to stay. My brother thinks I'll have a much better chance of getting a good husband in New York than in Bialystok! I hope he's right, but I've got my doubts."

"Why?"

"Well, just look at me, Sarah, I'm twenty five years old, I'm plain and …"

"You're not plain at all," Sarah interrupted, looking closely at Rosa's heart-shaped face. Her reddish brown hair was parted down the centre and shaped into a bun at the back of her head. Her hazel eyes twinkled when she laughed. "I think you're very pretty, Rosa."

"Me? Me pretty? Well that's a laugh, I'm sure!" Rosa scoffed.

"But you are," Sarah insisted. "You've got such lovely kind eyes. My Papa used to say that kind eyes are the window of the soul."

"Thanks for the compliment, Sarah," Rosa said giving her a quick hug. "Just the same, I know I'm not really much to look at. I'm poor, so I'm definitely not what is known as a 'good *shidduch* – a good match.' To be honest Sarah, I'm in no great hurry to get married. There'll be so much to do and to see before I think about settling down and raising a family. First off, I want to get a job, meet lots of people, make new friends and get used to living in a great city like New York."

"What kind of a job?"

"Sewing. We're all sewers in our family. I'm a seamstress and I'd love to learn about American women's fashion designs, and all the different new styles and fabrics I've heard about. Well, that's enough about me. You hungry?"

"Starving!"

"We'll get something to eat at the next station. I'm sure it won't be as good as the meals you shared with your friends and relations, but it'll be something to keep us going." She put her hand over Sarah's.

"Leave your money where it is," she whispered, "I'll pay. My father, God rest his soul, was a tailor and I sold his sewing machine. I know what you're thinking," Rosa giggled. "I don't think we'd have managed to get seats on this train if I'd had to carry his sewing machine! But here we are rattling along to Bremerhaven packed as tight as a barrel-full of herrings!"

★ ★ ★

Sarah had no idea how long she had slept when Rosa woke her.

"We're here! This is Bremerhaven!"

With a grinding of brakes followed by a shudder or two, the train hissed slowly to a halt. Carriage doors were flung open and crowds of weary travellers spilled out on to the platform. Sarah stood wide-eyed and open mouthed in astonishment.

"Just look at all those boats!" she gasped. Ships of every shape and size lay side by side gently bobbing up and down in the harbour. There were tall-masted sailing boats, massive steam ships, warships, fishing schooners and tugboats, many of them firmly secured by thick strong ropes fastened to great iron rings embedded in the walls or tied round metal posts at the edge of the water. The entire waterfront was gripped in a fever of activity: sea captains shouting orders, gangs of men loading and unloading barrels, crates and enormous wooden boxes on to carts and wagons. There were sailors everywhere, scrubbing the decks, dragging ropes and climbing the rigging. High above, thousands of screeching seagulls swooped and dived on fishing boats, or strutted about on the quayside pecking around the fisherwomen who were busy gutting herrings.

"SS *Werra*," Rosa announced.

"What?"

"That's the name of our ship. We've got to get our registration papers before we're allowed on board. See that big building over there? That's the Immigration Office. Come on. Let's hope it won't take all day."

The cold airless hall was packed with immigrants clutching their belongings. Sarah tried to ignore the knot of panic in the pit of her stomach.

"We're going too slowly, Rosa," she said nervously, looking at the long line of people waiting to have their papers checked. "We'll never get to the front of the line at this rate. What's going to happen if the boat leaves without us? I keep thinking about Aunt Manya waiting for me in New York and I'm ..."

"Enough already!" Rosa interrupted. "I'm not listening to that kind of talk, Sarah, d'you hear?" she said sternly. "What's got into you for goodness sake? We won't miss the boat. Believe me, there's no need to worry. The captain of the ship depends on our ticket money, you can bet on it. Look around you, child. D'you see? Most of his passengers are lining up here so he's going to have to wait for all of us however long it takes. "

"Sometimes I wonder why you put up with me!" Sarah sniffed. "I'm not very good at being patient am I?" she asked, fidgeting with her plaits. She could have cried with relief when finally it was their turn. Rosa sorted out their tickets and papers and handed them over to the Authorities Port Officers. When they were carefully checked, they were stamped and returned.

"What did I tell you? See?" Rosa said, waving the papers. "So let this be an end to all your worrying Sarah – alright?" She grabbed her hand and pulled her back through the crowd and out of the building. They had just reached the doorway when a tall man who was coming the other way bumped into them and accidentally knocked Sarah's bag out of her hand. It fell on the ground spilling all its contents.

"I'm very sorry," the man apologised. "It's my fault. I was in too much of a hurry. Here, let me help you," and without waiting for an answer, he stepped in front of Rosa, and began collecting Sarah's scattered belongings.

"Ah, yes, this is good, this is so good," he nodded, picking up Sarah's Hebrew prayer book and opening it up, hesitantly read out the words "Boris Nossovsky."

Sarah nodded. "I'm Sarah Nossovsky. It was my father's, God rest his soul, and it's mine now," she told him.

"And my name is Emanuel Mindel. Everyone calls me Manny," he smiled. "I know you'll always treasure your father's prayer book, Sarah. May I look at it for a moment? Yes?" He turned the pages slowly and carefully and then stopped and nodded. "Good. I've found it. Here is the prayer which travellers say before they go on a sea voyage."

"Will you read it for me and my friend Rosa please?" Sarah asked shyly. Manny smiled and nodded.

By this time a small crowd of people had gathered round to listen.

He began: "*They that go down to the sea in ships …*" and when he had finished everyone joined in with the '*Amens.*'

Manny closed the prayer book and handed it back to Sarah. "Thank you. My prayer books are safely packed away with my luggage," he told her. "If I hadn't bumped into you I wouldn't have had the chance to read this prayer. It's beshert!" He lingered for a moment, looking at them both. Then, making his way to the queue for the desk, he gave them a last smile. "See you on board!" he said.

Before I forget … Aunt Manya, I think Rosa has adopted me whatever that means! She's so kind and helpful and I couldn't have managed without her. She keeps telling me that I'm a brave girl. I don't really know what that means. I just keep going because I have no other choice, and, it's the only way I'll get to see you isn't it? Papa made this long journey and I'm just following in his footsteps! How strange that sounds! But it's true isn't it?

Chapter 6

Sarah's hands felt cold and damp as she grasped the iron railings of the gangway. The black hulk of the ship towered above her and a whiff of salty sea water far below made her nostrils tingle. She followed Rosa and the long line of passengers moving slowly up to the deck. Her heart was racing with excitement, but at the same time, deep down inside her, she couldn't help feeling just a little bit ...

"Scared? You scared?" A voice suddenly hissed in her ear and she felt hot breath on the back of her neck. It was as if somebody had read her most secret thoughts. She spun round quickly and came face to face with a pretty young girl who looked a few years older than herself. She had arched eyebrows over her black eyes, a pale skin, a decent shaped nose which, Sarah thought, she would happily have swapped with her own if she could, and black hair which reached her shoulders.

"Sorry, I didn't mean to make you jump. I just wanted to ask if you were feeling a bit scared," the girl explained with a friendly smile.

"Well, sort of 'yes' and sort of 'no'," Sarah replied thoughtfully. "I'm all churned up inside."

"I guess I am too 'cause I've never been on a boat before. My name's Perle Rosen, by the way. What's yours?"

"Sarah Nossovsky."

"Where's your family?"

"My parents are dead and I'm going to New York to live with my Aunt Manya. She'll be waiting for me in Ellis Island."

"What?" Perle gasped in surprise. "You're all on your own?!"

"I'm not now. I met Rosa, thank goodness, who has sort of adopted me." She tugged at Rosa's sleeve and grinned. "This is Perle."

Rosa smiled. "Glad to meet you, Perle. You by yourself too?"

Perle shook her head. "No. I'm with my two cousins. They're behind me down the line somewhere. I'm going to live with my older sister in New York. She's expecting a baby soon and my mother sent me to help her."

"Where you from?" Rosa asked.

"From Oldenburg in Germany. It's about forty or fifty miles from here I think. Oh! Look up there!" They followed her gaze to the end of the line. "There's a sailor handing out something. It looks like bundles of straw, and a sort of bowl."

"What are they for?" Sarah asked.

"The straw will be for our beds I think, and the bowl

thing's to get water." Perle was right. When Sarah reached the top of the gangway and stepped on to the deck, a bundle of straw, a thin quilt and a tin bowl with a handle was pushed roughly into her arms. The man pointed and said something to her.

"I don't understand. What's he's saying, Perle?"

"He's speaking German. He said, 'Steerage; women this way and men down there.' "

"What's steerage?"

"Dunno. We'd best follow Rosa and find out."

They went down some narrow steps, their footsteps echoing on the metal rungs. The air was stale and musty. They followed a dark narrow corridor to a long, windowless, low-ceilinged room fitted with wooden shelves, one above the other. It was packed from end to end with women: young and old, tall and short, dark and fair. Many of them were dressed in shabby black skirts, others in brightly coloured dresses and aprons, flowered headscarves and embroidered shawls. Some were trying to pacify their screaming babies and others cradled sleeping ones. There were women sitting on the floor, on boxes, on suitcases, and on bundles of quilts and blankets. Some were praying, some crying, and most were shouting, quarrelling and arguing, not just in Yiddish, but in many strange languages Sarah had never heard before. She felt her stomach churn from the smell of sweaty bodies, and worse still, her nostrils curled at the terrible stench of ... well, she thought, it was as if everyone had just wet themselves.

Sarah held her nose. "What a terrible stink! I think I'm going to be sick."

"These are our bunk beds," Rosa told her. "At least we've got some straw to lie on, and even a bit of a quilt to cover ourselves."

"Beds? I thought they were shelves," Sarah muttered.

"It'll be a bit of a squeeze to get in and out. I pity anyone who's fat!" Perle grinned.

"There's nowhere private," Sarah snapped, looking away from a woman breast-feeding her baby. "There's no room to move and I can't breathe in here. How are we going to live in all this crowd and noise and dirt and mess for days on end, or even for weeks?"

"We'll do what everyone else is doing, Sarah," Rosa said quietly, looking at her reproachfully. "We'll manage. We won't starve and dirt can always be washed off, you know."

Sarah felt ashamed. She put her hands on her flushed cheeks.

"Oh Rosa, I'm so sorr ..." Her words were drowned in a sudden deafening blast from the ship's siren, the engines burst into life with a loud throbbing noise vibrating from under the floorboards. The ship began to move.

"We're off! We're really moving," Perle shouted. "I'm going up on deck to see what's going on. You coming, Sarah?"

"Rosa, I didn't mean to ... I ... I ..." she stopped, turned away and ran after Perle.

Everyone, it seemed, had the same idea! Hundreds of passengers were jostling for a place along the ship's rails for a last glance of the Bremerhaven coastline. By the time Sarah found Perle, the fluttering handkerchiefs, the cheering, waving crowds lining the waterfront were slowly fading into the distance.

"I wish Joseph and Malka could have been waving to me," she sighed. "I hope they are safe. I miss them and I miss Vaska too," she whispered quietly to herself so Perle couldn't hear.

"In case you want to know, the North Sea and the North Atlantic Ocean are between us and the Immigration Port of

Ellis Island in New York," Perle announced. "What's up?" she asked, looking at Sarah's tight lips and pale face. "Are you upset or something?"

"I feel so awful. I got into a bad temper and I had no right to talk to Rosa like that. I shouldn't have complained. She'll think I'm … I'm … I dunno what she's going to think of me." She bit her bottom lip and brushed tears away with the back of her hand.

"Oh, come on Sarah. You don't have to feel so bad. Rosa isn't stupid. She'll understand. Everyone in steerage knows it's a hell-hole down there."

"I know that," Sarah sniffed. "I've just escaped from a different sort of 'hell-hole', as you call it. I've got no right to complain about this one!"

"How do you mean – escaped?"

Sarah watched the white crests of the waves slap, slapping against the side of the ship before she answered. "My stepmother didn't love me and made my life a misery. I can put up with anything now that I know I'll never see her again."

"Good for you. Come to think of it," Perle said thoughtfully, "I've escaped too, in a way."

"You have?" Sarah asked. "How d'you mean?"

"Oh not like you. Nothing like that. Just the same, I reckon I got away just in time."

"Got away?" Sarah repeated.

"I was beginning to feel trapped. As soon as I turned sixteen, I noticed that my mother and my aunts were starting to whisper about me behind my back."

"What about?"

"They never told me but I guessed they were making plans to marry me off young, like a lot of my friends. I'm not soft up here, y'know," Perle said, tapping the side of her head. "I had a good idea what was going on."

"What?"

"Well, for one thing, whenever the Rabbi called at our house, he brought his nineteen-year-old son with him."

"Oh, I get it," Sarah grinned, "he was to be your husband, your 'intended'. Was he a good *shidduch* – a good match?"

"Ugh!" Perle shuddered and pulled a face. "He was pale and spotty, and didn't say a word. Talk about being afraid of his own shadow! I'm so glad I've escaped from all that. Hannah won't try to marry me off. She's very modern, you know, and so is Abe her husband. They're determined to be good Americans and when their baby is born they've decided to speak to it in English. So I'll tell you what, Sarah," she said earnestly. "If they can learn English, so can we!"

"English?"

"Now what are you girls up to?" Rosa asked when she joined them. "Did I hear you mention something about learning English? Yes? Good. Can I join the class? 'There's no time like now,' my dear Papa used to say. Anyone hungry? I am, so follow me and we'll see what food there is on offer."

"Rosa," Sarah hesitated. "Rosa," she began again. "I just want to …"

Rosa bent down and put her arm round Sarah's shoulders. "It's OK. Save your breath, child," she whispered. *Rosa's forgiven me*, Sarah thought. *I know she has. I can tell from the way she looks at me with her kind eyes. From now on, Sarah Nossovsky, no more whining and no more complaining. You'll just have to manage down below in steerage like everyone else.*

Supper, which consisted of herrings, potatoes and thick slices of black bread, didn't take long to eat.

"D'you know what my friend Joseph would say?" Sarah

asked, playing with some left over bread crumbs. "That was the kind of meal you won't want to remember in a hurry!"

"You're right, Sarah," Perle grinned. "But I think it's the kind of food we'll have to get used to! Look, we're not needed here," Perle said, watching Rosa who was busy helping a woman with her three little children. "I'm going to get some fresh air. You coming?" Sarah followed her to the small deck allocated for steerage passengers. The boat swayed from side to side and end to end in the choppy waters and they soon learned to grab hold of rails or each other to keep their balance. They were deep in conversation when suddenly, out of nowhere, a beautiful soft shawl floated down right over Sarah's head!

"Where on earth did this come from," Sarah laughed as she pulled it off her face. "Just look at it. Have you ever seen anything as beautiful as this? Feel it. It's so soft, I think it's made of silk. And all these bright colours, blue and pink and gold and …"

"Sarah!" Perle interrupted. "Look up there! Someone's waving to us!"

A woman was standing on the deck above them shouting something the girls couldn't understand.

"I don't know what she's saying but I think the shawl must belong to her. I think she wants us to bring it up – see, she keeps pointing over there."

"How can we? You know we're not allowed up there – that's in First Class."

"First Class or not," Perle snapped with a toss of her head. "We've had an invitation to go up there, so we're going. Come on!"

"We might get into trouble. Are you sure it'll be alright?" There was no answer. Perle had gone. Sarah had no choice but to follow her, climbing steps and striding along corridors.

"I think this is the cabin," Perle whispered. "Let's hope I'm right," she said as she tapped on the door. They almost held their breath while they waited for the door to open and were relieved to see that it was the same woman. She took the silk scarf and nodded and smiled and invited them into her cabin, which – Sarah couldn't help noticing – she had all to herself! The woman spoke to them in a language she didn't understand.

"What is she saying, Perle?" Sarah asked. "She's not speaking Yiddish, that's for sure. Is it German?"

It was and Sarah watched them chatting together. "What are you two talking about, Perle? I'm dying to know!"

"The woman's name is Mrs Jensen. She comes from Norway but she's been living with relatives in Germany," Perle explained. "She must be very clever because she can speak German, English and French as well as her native Norwegian. She thanks us both very much for returning her shawl."

Mrs Jensen smiled and offered the girls a plate of delicious white rolls filled with cheese.

"This is much better food than we get in steerage, isn't it?" Sarah said quietly. "Did you say she can speak English?"

"Yes."

"D'you think you could ask her to teach us and Rosa some English? She seems such a nice lady, I don't think she'll mind."

Perle asked her and from the vigorous nodding and chatting and smiling it was clear that Mrs Jensen was very pleased with the idea.

When Rosa first heard the news she frowned.

"Are you sure about all this?" she asked. "I mean to say that…"

"Mrs Jensen said she really wants to do it, Rosa," Perle interrupted. "She can't wait to start. She's even going to get official permission for us to come to her cabin for our lessons."

"Well, if you're sure we won't be a nuisance or a burden on her, we must make the most of her kindness. It's not going to be easy," Rosa warned them, "but I think we should give it a try."

Lesson one! Mrs Jensen gave each of them a pencil and a sheet of SS *Werra* headed paper on which she had written a short list of simple English words. She read them out in German for Perle who translated everything into Yiddish for Sarah and Rosa.

"This is the most 'unstraightforward' method of teaching I've ever seen!" Sarah laughed.

"Round about or not," Rosa said. "It'll work just so long as we're determined to learn. By the way," she smiled, "guess what? I've just elected myself as the new Homework Supervisor!"

They did their best to concentrate on this new language until, little by little, their knowledge of English improved. They soon discovered that Mrs Jensen was not easily satisfied. They had to work hard on their list of English words before they were given a new one together with some short sentences.

"What's that you're scribbling away at, Sarah?" Perle asked when they were busy with homework.

"Well, it's …" she hesitated.

"It's what?"

"It's a very short note which I've written to Aunt Manya. I'll keep it in my bag and read it out to her when I see her."

"Good girl. Show me."

Deer Ont Manya,

Mis Jensen is tiching me and my frends Rosa and Perle to lerning Inglish so I can tork you in New York. Rosa meks us do homwork. It is very hod.
Love from Sarah.

"She'll love it, Sarah. Honestly she will," Perle grinned. "And what's more she's going to keep it and treasure it."

Before I forget … dreams are such strange things aren't they, Aunt Manya? We don't order them, they just come whether we like them or not. I had such a vivid dream last night. I was in the wagon with Mama and Papa and the sun was shining and we were singing together. Then we stopped for a picnic – guess where? In a field of bright red poppies!

Chapter 7

"Wake up!" a voice suddenly hissed in Sarah's ear. "Can you hear me, child, wake up!" She felt a strong hand shaking her as she struggled to open her eyes.

"Rosa! What's up? What's the matter?"

"Hush, get up and don't make a noise. I need you and Perle to help me. It's urgent."

Rubbing her eyes and stifling a yawn Sarah slid out of her bed. Perle, who looked as if she too had just woken up, came and stood next to her.

"What's going on?" she asked.

"Esther, one of the women here, is having a baby – right now."

"Now?" Sarah gasped. "A baby being born on the ship? What . . ?"

"Shush!" Rosa held up her hand. "This is no time for questions. I've been up all night with her and I'm tired. Are you going to help me?"

The girls nodded.

"Good. I've screened off a corner of the washroom for her so she can have a bit of privacy. She needs a comfortable bed. Go and find some kind sailors – the older ones understand better – and ask them for some fresh straw, quilts, pieces of canvas, clean shirts or anything clean we can cut up, and lots of hot water. Here," Rosa handed Perle a storm lantern. "You'll need this."

"But it's the middle of the night and …"

"Wake the men up if necessary. Just do your best," Rosa snapped and disappeared into the wash room.

"How does she expect me to wake up snoring sailors, for goodness sake," Perle muttered in a low voice.

"D'you know where they sleep?" Sarah asked nervously.

"No I don't. I chat to some of the German sailors now and again when they're on duty, but I've no idea where their quarters are."

"You're very good at finding your way around." Sarah murmured, trying hard to sound positive.

The lantern cast long odd-shaped shadows as they climbed up the metal steps on to the wind-swept deck. Sarah looked up at the starry sky above them. She raised her arm to point out the brightest one when she was suddenly startled by the appearance of a tall figure holding a lantern who appeared out of the shadows. He called out to them in a gruff voice.

"Who is he, for goodness sake? What's he saying, Perle?" she gasped clinging fast to the railings.

"He wants to know what we're doing here."

"Are you going to tell him?"

"I have to."

Sarah watched them talking to each other. "What's happening?" she asked.

"He said we're lucky to have come to the right man and he'll do his best to get everything on Rosa's list," Perle translated. "Not only is he the Senior Officer on duty tonight but he's a married man and understands the situation, which a lot of the young crew don't. He told me something else too," Perle said gravely.

"What?"

"During his last voyage to America two babies died. Well it's hardly surprising because the conditions in steerage are bad enough for us let alone for new born babies."

Sarah swallowed hard. "Oh I'm so sorry for those poor little babies. What happened to them?"

"Each one was wrapped in a sheet of canvas, a few prayers were said, and then they were lowered overboard. There was just no other choice," Perle sighed.

"Will Esther's baby die too?" Sarah asked brushing away the tears that were rolling down her cheeks.

"Not if we can help it."

Sarah sniffed, swallowed hard and pulled her shawl tightly round her to keep out the cold. "I hope he comes soon," she shivered. Their luck was in and they didn't have long to wait. The officer returned with two big parcels and a bucket of hot water which he carried down to steerage.

He placed the bucket on the floor, muttered something to Perle and left before they had a chance to thank him.

"He's gone to make his rounds of the decks," she told Sarah. "He said to let him know if we want anything else."

"Good girls, thank you," Rosa smiled, as she collected the parcels and picked up the bucket. "You must have found a real mensch."

Rosa and two other women seemed to be in charge of looking after Esther. A strong smell of disinfectant – used to clean the washroom floor – made Sarah's nostrils twitch.

"Esther was hoping to have her baby in America, not on a boat in the middle of the Atlantic Ocean. It can't be helped," she shrugged, "I've been told that babies don't conform to any plan. They're a law unto themselves." Suddenly they heard loud screams coming from inside the washroom.

"Oh Rosa, whatever's happening in there?"

"Don't be frightened, Sarah. It's only natural for Esther to be in a lot of pain. It will all be forgotten from the moment her baby is born."

"From the moment her baby is born," Sarah repeated. "Where is Esther going to put the baby?" she asked herself. And then an idea flashed into her head so suddenly, it made her body tingle with excitement.

Just then, Rosa shouted, "Perle bring me two of those tin bowls with a handle and…"

"I want her to come and help me get something for the baby," Sarah butted in. She whispered something to Perle and they were just about to leave when Rosa called them back.

"Whatever it is, it must wait. Perle is needed here."

"I'm sorry," Perle whispered, squeezing Sarah's hand. "You can see what it's like down here. Go and find that officer and remember what I told you to ask for: *Eine wiege für das baby* – a cradle for the baby. It's a great idea which I don't think anyone else has got round to thinking about."

"I do hope that nice officer will still be on duty," Sarah muttered as she climbed the steps again. A streak of morning light was just breaking through the clouds – enough to see by. "The search is on!" she said loud enough to give her courage. With her heart in her mouth she trailed along endless dark passages looking for the kind officer. "What am I going to do if I bump into someone else?" she said to herself. "It won't be any use trying to explain because he won't understand. I'm frightened that ..." She stopped abruptly at a sudden turn in the passage which led to some steps. She climbed them quickly and found herself on a deck. "I've no idea where I am. I'm lost and I think I'm going to scream or cry or both!" Before she had time to do either she saw the officer standing on the deck above. She shouted and waved her arms to attract his attention. He saluted, disappeared and finally appeared close by.

Sarah wasted no time. She burst out: "*Eine wiege für das baby!*" and watched his face closely to see if he understood what she was saying. To her great relief he smiled and nodded. He signalled her to follow him to a large storeroom in a far corner of the deck. It was packed from floor to ceiling with tools, machine parts, wooden boxes and crates of all sizes, long planks of decking, sheets of canvas and sacks of sawdust.

The officer pulled down a large wooden box which he offered to Sarah.

She shook her head. "I know you're trying to help, but I don't know how to tell you it's much too big! *Eine wiege für das baby!*" Sarah repeated as she kept up her search. At last, tired and dirty, she almost shouted for joy when she noticed, partly concealed behind a roll of canvas, a small wooden barrel. It immediately sparked a vivid memory of Papa in his workshop with a small wooden barrel which he sawed in half vertically. "Look at this, Sarah. Two little rocking cradles for the price of one!" he had laughed.

She tugged the officer's sleeve. "This one, this one," she said excitedly pointing to the barrel and indicating that he should pull it out for her. "I wish Perle was here," she said quietly. "How am I going to ask him to cut it down," she sighed, playing with her plaits. The solution came in a most unexpected way. She grabbed a few handfuls of sawdust, scattered it on the floor and with her finger traced the outline of the barrel. She had almost got to drawing the next stage of the operations when the officer smiled and nodded his head. "Ya, ya, gut, gut!" he chortled and patted Sarah on the head. The rest was easy. The officer found the tools he needed, split the barrel down and selected one of the halves with a firm base. Then, without Sarah having to ask, he lined it first with canvas, then straw and finally a piece of clean sacking.

She suddenly remembered that Perle had taught her how to say 'thank you' in German. "Danke, danke," she told him.

He nodded, smiled, patted Sarah on the head again, and was about to carry it down for her when Perle appeared bursting with news.

"Esther has a little girl! She's going to call her Golda. I'm just going to tell Mrs. Jensen and …" she stopped mid-sentence. She took one look at the wooden rocking cradle, grabbed Sarah by the waist and whirled her round. "Oh, Sarah! It's just perfect! You've worked miracles, you really have," she said, panting for breath. "Esther will love it and it'll be the best present she'll ever have." She shook hands with the officer and thanked him for which they both received a pat on the head!

The screened off 'baby' section of the washroom was a hub of activity. Sarah had never seen anything like it before. Rosa and her friends were busy clearing away soiled sheets and cloths and replacing smelly straw with a fresh supply. Esther, looking pale, exhausted and very happy, was holding baby Golda in her arms. Sarah just kept on staring at the sweet little face framed in a halo of curly black hair, blue eyes and tiny perfectly formed fingers and toes.

"*Mazel tov* – congratulations Esther! She is the most beautiful little baby I've ever seen in my whole life. I hope she'll like this," Sarah said shyly pointing to the cradle.

Esther gently lowered the baby in to the cradle and smiled. "It's wonderful, Sarah, and you can see for yourself how comfortable she is. I just don't know where to begin to thank you. What a kind thoughtful girl you are. Do you know why I've called her Golda?"

Sarah shook her head.

"The name Golda will always remind me of *De Goldene Medina*, 'The Golden Land of America.' This tiny baby will be amongst the first of a new generation to grow up in a free country without the threat of persecution. What a blessing she'll be to me and my husband who will be waiting for us."

There was a steady stream of women who came to see Esther and the new baby, admire the rocking cradle, bring little gifts and offer congratulations spoken in many different languages. "Even if Esther can't understand them all," she whispered, "I'm sure she knows what they mean."

Before I forget … such excitement last night, Aunt Manya! A tiny beautiful baby called Golda was born in the middle of the Atlantic Ocean! It must have been very hard for Esther to have a baby in steerage. This baby has changed us all. Everyone is in a good mood because of her, and there's not so much shouting and quarrelling. Golda has made me feel quite grown up. Isn't it amazing what a tiny baby can do!

Chapter 8

A storm was brewing. Sarah and Perle clung to the railings and watched the tossing waves and the black clouds racing across the sky.

"Come on down, girls," Rosa shouted against the wind. "There's going to be a storm. It's not safe on deck."

"I'm feeling seasick, Rosa. I'll suffocate down there. I'm much better off up here."

"Don't talk crazy. You can't stay here. You'll get washed overboard. The wind's getting stronger. Come down now. Be quick! Hurry up! I'm getting wet."

The steerage was in chaos. The rolling of the ship sent pots and pans flying, boxes and bundles slid across the dirty floor, babies were screaming, children staggering and falling, and those who weren't seasick were moaning or praying. The stench of vomit was overwhelming.

"Oh, God, I'm going to be sick," Sarah muttered as she felt her stomach heave. She tried hard to swallow. "I've got to get out of here, Rosa."

"It's too dangerous, Sarah, you'll …"

"I DON'T CARE!" Sarah shouted defiantly. "I CAN'T STAY HERE LISTENING TO EVERYONE RETCHING AND BEING SICK. I CAN'T STAND THE NOISE. IT STINKS IN HERE AND … AND … I JUST CAN'T STAND IT ANY MORE."

Sarah stood shaking after her sudden outburst, then, with her hand clutched tightly over her mouth, she stepped over loose boxes and parcels and ran back on deck to get to the railings just in time to throw up into the sea. The effort left her weak and gasping, but deep breaths of the bracing salt sea air soon cleared her head. As she stood gripping the rails, the storm clouds changed with terrifying speed. The wind howled and shrieked as it whipped round her body, nearly ripping off her shawl. The ship was creaking, groaning, rolling and shuddering from end to end. The whole sea erupted into inky black towering waves which crashed over her and sent her reeling. She remembered swerving to ward off a heavy blow from something. After that there was nothing – the entire world was silent and black – black.

★ ★ ★

Sarah heard a groan. *Was that me?* she thought. Another groan. *Yes, it's me.* She managed to open one eye then closed it again quickly.

Don't do that again, Sarah, she scolded, *not yet anyway, it's too painful!* Another groan when she tried to move. *Keep still then it won't hurt so much.*

She felt a kiss on her forehead and her hands being gently stroked.

"*Oy vey*, oh dear, you poor child," she heard Rosa mutter over and over again. "Don't try to open your eyes."

"What happened? Where am I?" she managed to mutter, wincing with pain.

"You are in Mrs Jensen's cabin and being well looked after. What a kind lady she is. She even sent for the ship's doctor to come and see you. Imagine that! What a time you've had, you poor thing. Take this medicine Sarah, and get some more rest. We'll talk when you're feeling better."

It took another two whole days before Sarah could open both her eyes without pain and Rosa judged her to be well on the road to recovery.

"Mmmm," she murmured, cupping Sarah's face in her hands and gently turning it from side to side. "Yes, much better," she announced.

"What happened? I remember feeling so ill and seasick I just had to get up on deck. I was very rude to shout at you."

"Dear child," Rosa sighed, "I don't blame you for wanting to throw up into the sea. The steerage was a stinking hell-hole what with everyone feeling ill and vomiting all over the place. Perle and I went crazy looking for you. I was out of my mind with worry. I was desperate because I thought you'd been washed overboard. I was going to ask the Captain to turn the boat round and search for you when Mrs. Jensen sent a message to tell me and Perle what happened." She blew her nose very hard. "Thank God for Manny," she sniffed.

"Manny?"

Rosa nodded. "His name is Emanuel but everyone calls him Manny. You met him. Don't you remember? He bumped into you in the Immigration Office when you dropped your bag."

Sarah nodded.

"Well," Rosa smiled, "Manny is the young man who saved your life! He was on deck with a few other passengers because he was feeling very sick too. D'you know what I keep saying over and over again?"

"No."

"Thank God a thousand times for Manny – a real mensch. You were knocked down by a piece of uprooted decking, and he ran to pick you up. He was just going to carry you downstairs when Mrs Jensen, who saw it all, shouted to him to bring you up to her cabin. He's been here every day to find out how you are. It's no wonder you're in pain from that terrible fall – concussion, two black eyes, a cut lip, two cracked ribs, and a sprained ankle. It'll all heal up in good time but you must be patient."

"Fancy waking up in bed with real sheets!" Sarah winced – her cut lip hurt too much to smile. Just then the cabin door opened and Mrs Jensen came in followed by Manny and Perle.

Sarah sat up slowly with a groan. "Perle, please thank Mrs Jensen for looking after me so well. Tell her we've got to start our lessons again when I'm better. I want to be able to thank her properly in English." She looked at Manny. "You saved my life," she said shyly. "And I really don't know how to begin to thank you."

Manny gripped her hand. "I'm very glad I was in the right place at the right time," he smiled, placing a kiss on the top of her head. "Get well soon, Sarah. I'm sure your Aunt Manya won't want to see you with two black eyes!"

Before I forget ... I'll tell you all about the terrible storm when I see you, Aunt Manya. I am sick and tired of rocking and bouncing about all the time. Do you know what I want more than anything else in the world – apart from seeing you, of course? I WANT TO STAND QUITE STILL ON DRY LAND!

Chapter 9

Sarah managed to squeeze herself between two piles of thick ropes – a good shelter from the wind and even more importantly – a private hiding place. She chewed on her pencil and read her second letter.

SS Werra

Dear Ont Manya,

I fell and hert me. I am better. I lernt lots more English. Mrs Jensen is good teacher. She toks me in English. She says things slow so I can understand wot she said. I want to go to school because I love to lerning. Love from Sarah.

"It's no use," she grumbled as she folded it up and put it in her bag. "I can't do anymore." She shook her head and frowned. "I don't know what's got into me today, but I can't seem to put my mind to anything." She watched the spray bursting over the deck as the tossing waves hit the side of the boat. She looked at the vast ocean that stretched all around her as far as the distant horizon.

Sometimes I feel we're just drifting in the middle of all this emptiness. There's nothing to see, nothing to look at – just more and more of this vast empty ocean. My head is full of questions which won't go away. How many more days in steerage? Will Aunt Manya find out when our boat arrives? Will she be there to meet me? Will she? Please God, will she? When will we get to Ellis Island? I'm sick of people telling me over and over again, "We'll be there soon." How long is soon? That's what I want to know. Come to think of it, that's what every single person on this ship wants to know.

"There you are!" Rosa laughed. "Dear God in heaven, I'm getting grey hairs chasing after you. Look what I've got," she said, waving a small package.

"What is it?"

"Stale cheese!"

"Cheese?"

"Yes, cheese! The first class passengers turned up their noses at it, would you believe. One of those kind German sailors gave it to Perle and she's been busy sharing it out. I've cut away the mouldy bits. The black bread's stale too, I'm afraid, so mind you chew it well. Eat, eat already, you don't want your Aunt Manya to think I've been starving you, do you?"

That first bite reminded Sarah just how hungry she was. "Stale or not it still tastes of cheese," she said with her mouth full.

"My dear child," Rosa lowered her voice as if she was embarrassed. "I've got something very important to tell you. I want you to know," Rosa hesitated, then she went on. "I want you to know," she repeated, "that you've changed my life."

Sarah's mouth opened wide in surprise, and bits of bread dropped on to her skirt. Was she seeing things? Rosa was blushing!

"How? I don't understand. What d'you mean? " she asked, busily picking up the stray breadcrumbs.

"Well. Well you see …" Rosa stopped, then explained. "You remember when Manny saved you from being washed overboard? He … well, he was so worried about you. He kept calling to see how you were and little by little we … I mean, he … and I …" Rosa's blush deepened. A secret smile hovered over her lips.

Sarah's eyes grew wider. "Oh! I get it!" she cried. "You two got to know each other. *Really* got to know each other, I mean," she grinned.

Rosa nodded shyly. "We got talking about you, of course, and how lucky it was that he was on deck too in that terrible storm. Then we had a friendly chat about sewing and tailoring and the fact that we're both from Bialystok. And it turned out that he knows one of my cousins. Not all that well, but enough to get us chatting about our families and who we knew and who we didn't." She stopped and smiled as if she was enjoying just thinking about it.

"Oh, Rosa, you look so happy and Manny is a real mensch. Are you going to get married? Is he a 'good catch' or is it a 'good match'?" she asked innocently. She turned round suddenly to see Manny smiling down at her.

"A 'good catch' or 'a good match'?" he said thoughtfully, sitting down beside her. "I don't know about that, Sarah.

I'm just a poor tailor hoping to find work and a new life in America. Rosa and I have what's called 'an understanding.' As soon as we get jobs we'll start saving up to get married. And we both can't help thinking that if you hadn't been a bit crazy and ..."

"And disobeyed Rosa," Sarah butted in.

"Oh, Sarah," Rosa murmured, her eyes were sparkling with joy. "It sounds a dreadful thing to say, but if you hadn't gone back on deck, even though you were in danger, Manny and I wouldn't have got to know each other so well. Oh, I nearly forgot. This is for you," she said, handing her a second parcel.

"For me?" Sarah's eyes sparkled with pleasure as she opened the parcel and found a smart canvas bag decorated with her initials stitched in red ribbon.

"D'you like it?" Rosa asked.

"Do I like it?" Sarah repeated, swallowing hard. "What a question! It's much nicer than my flour sack and has a much longer strap to go over my shoulder," she said tracing round the initials S.N. with her finger. "It's beautiful. Thank you both very much."

"Manny made it out of a spare piece of canvas one of the sailors gave him," Rosa explained proudly. "And I stitched on your initials with the red ribbon Mrs Jensen gave me. We've all put a little something in it for you."

Sarah emptied the contents of the bag and apart from her few personal items of clothing, she found a notebook and two pencils from Mrs Jensen, a pretty handkerchief from Rosa, and Perle had made a list of her family and all her friends' addresses, carefully written in English on the ship's notepaper.

"Well," Rosa said quietly looking at Sarah's trembling lips. "I think that's enough excitement for one day, don't you? If we can grab a clean space in the washroom, I'll wash your hair. And if there's any leftovers, how about some more bread and stale cheese for supper, eh?"

"Sarah, I hope you realise that in spite of all the aches and pains you suffered, you've brought Rosa and me together and given us a happy future together. You know what I think?" Manny asked her.

Sarah thought for a moment then she looked up at him with a big smile.

"Yes, I know exactly what you think! It was meant to happen – it's beshert isn't it?"

"Well of course it is! It's beshert!" Manny laughed and gave them both a kiss.

Before I forget … Ugghh! I had my very first tiny taste of whisky today, Aunt Manya. It made me cough and splutter! Mrs. Jensen made a little party for Rosa and Manny because they are sort of engaged. Manny taught her the Hebrew toast: 'L'Chaim!' which means 'your good health.' He also taught her to say: 'Mazel tov' – 'congratulations'. Perle and I were more interested in eating lots of delicious little cakes!

Chapter 10

Excitement swept through steerage with the speed of a forest fire. Instead of the usual bickering and noisy arguments, everyone, even the fretful children, was in a happy mood, bustling about, laughing and chattering as they packed up their belongings. Blankets, feather quilts, pillows, prayer books, candlesticks, clothes and all the rest of their precious possessions were tied up in huge bundles or stuffed into big leather cases, wicker baskets, boxes and bags and every other available piece of luggage.

"That's another good job done," Rosa said, tidying her hair and brushing down her skirt.

"What is?" Sarah asked.

"Oh didn't I tell you? I got Perle to give a message to the nice officer who, thanks to you Sarah, made Golda's cradle.

He's fixed a strong leather strap on it so that Esther can carry it off the boat. And before you ask me, Golda is doing just fine. She does occasionally get mixed up about feeding times, but luckily I don't have to get up in the middle of the night!" she laughed. "You know what, Sarah," she said, looking round the room. "This place looks just like the Tower of Babel in the Bible. Thank goodness we're travelling light. I can't wait to get out of here. Come on, let's go."

The steerage deck was crammed from end to end. Hundreds of passengers, immigrants from all over the world, stood squashed together staring into the distance for their first glimpse of America.

Sarah felt a kiss on her cheek followed by a big hug from Perle. "I have to go with my cousins otherwise we'll get separated in this crowd. Goodbye Sarah. You've got the list of addresses haven't you? Yes? Good. We'll write to each other."

"In English?"

"What else!" she grinned. She kissed Rosa, shook hands with Manny and was soon lost in the crowd.

"Look over there!" Manny shouted, pointing in the direction of a grey smudge on the horizon. All eyes were focused on the distant shoreline and when the ship got close enough to see more clearly, the passengers went wild with joy.

"America! *De Goldene Medina, The Golden Land*," they shouted over and over again. They danced and cried and prayed and hugged and kissed each other and sang until they were hoarse.

Cheers went up again as they sailed past the breathtaking sight of the tallest statue Sarah had ever seen. *It's almost touching heaven*, she thought.

"Do you know who that is?" Manny asked her. Sarah shook her head.

"It's called the Statue of Liberty," he explained. "It's supposed to represent the Roman Goddess of freedom. Every immigrant, like us, will see her when they sail to America. It's a fine symbol of freedom to be placed at the gateway of a free country, don't you think Sarah?" She just nodded, much too excited to speak.

And then, at long last, it happened. The constant throb of the engines stopped as suddenly as it had begun when the boat left Bremerhaven.

"We're here! We've arrived!" Sarah shouted out to anyone who would listen. Memories came flooding back to the time when she'd first spoken to Perle as they climbed aboard the *SS Werra*. She leaned over the railings to watch the sailors lower the gangways. Then the long slow stream of shuffling, scruffy passengers, weighed down with all their belongings, began to disembark from the boat. The Immigration Registry Room on Ellis Island was waiting for them.

Little by little the happy mood changed to one of worry and anxiety. Sarah stood staring, trying hard to take it all in. The Registry Room was a vast hall divided into long rows where the immigrants lined up for inspection.

"What a place! I've never seen such a big room in all my life," she whispered to Rosa. "It must be as big as the ship."

"Listen carefully, child," Rosa said gently, cupping Sarah's face in her hands. "In case we get separated I want you to remember everything I tell you. Keep calm and don't do anything crazy. D'you see all those men in uniforms? Look! At the top of the stairs? Yes? Well they're Medical Inspectors. Walk nice and straight up the stairs. Don't stoop, otherwise they might think there's something wrong with you and won't let you through. After the medical exams another inspector will ask you some questions. If you don't understand all the English, there'll be someone there who'll translate for you.

Remember, the man will ask the questions, not you, so don't interrupt him and don't argue. You're fit and well, and your papers are all in order so you've got nothing to worry about. D'you hear me?"

Sarah nodded. "Aren't you and Manny coming to meet my Aunt Manya?"

Rosa shook her head. "It's kind of you to think about us but I'm quite sure your Aunt will want you all to herself. Besides I'll be looking out for my family. I can't wait to introduce my 'good catch'," Rosa murmured, smiling at Manny.

He gave Sarah a bear like hug. "God bless you, brave girl. I'll tell you something. As soon as we're all settled we're going to celebrate with a big 'get-together' and I promise that you will be our special guest of honour!"

Everything happened just as Rosa had said. It was when she started to straighten her back that she suddenly thought of Papa. "He was here," she said under her breath. "I know what he would have told me: 'Straight back, Sarah, and no slouching!' I think 'slouching' was one of his favourite words!" At the top of the stairs the Medical Inspectors were busy examining people one after the other in quick succession. Sarah joined a line of women waiting their turn to see the doctor. She watched him examine one of the women, take a piece of chalk and write the letter 'E' on the back of her jacket. Rosa had told her that the 'E' stood for a serious eye disease and anyone who had it was sent back. Then something happened which Sarah knew she was not supposed to have seen. She gasped and put her hand over her mouth as she watched the poor sobbing woman with E on her back being led away into the crowd by her husband. Then quick as a flash, he took off her jacket, turned it inside out and helped her to put it on again.

Sarah lost count of the number of times she told herself to keep calm during that long boring day. Finally, after much poking and prodding she passed the medical exams and moved on to another inspector. He sat on a high stool with a Yiddish interpreter at his side. She answered most of the questions, although some were too difficult even when translated into Yiddish. When it was finished the inspector wrote 'SARAH NOSSOVSKY' in large letters on a piece of card, attached it to a piece of string and hung it round her neck. "So your Aunt will know who you are!" he said in English, and, with a nod of approval, put his official stamp on her papers.

"Tank you, tank you, sir," she stuttered, shaking like a leaf with excitement. She looked round at the thousands of excited immigrants milling about the great hall. "Rosa and Manny are somewhere in there. I wish I could show them this," she murmured as she fingered her name card. "They'll be so happy for me." She found a quiet corner where she could sit and wait and watch. Not long afterwards she was joined by an old couple who sat down wearily on their boxes.

"How tired you look, child," the woman clucked kindly, handing her a piece of her bread. "Here, *gesundheit* – eat it in good health!" Sarah thanked her, and ate ravenously, collecting any leftover crumbs then, using her new canvas bag as a pillow, she lay down and promptly fell asleep.

"Sarah Nossovsky?" Sarah opened her eyes and saw a man in uniform standing over her.

"Sarah Nossovsky?" he repeated.

She sat up with a start and looked around. Apart from a few stragglers, the vast room was almost empty.

"Yes. I Sarah Nossovsky," she answered, quickly getting to her feet.

"Come with me," he said in English.

"Where we go?"

No reply.

"Plis tell me where we go now?" she asked again in English.

The man shook his head and gestured for her to follow him.

Sarah's mind was bursting with a million questions she was too scared to ask. Who is this man? Where is he taking me? Has Aunt Manya come and gone? Has she missed her? Perhaps she'd come looking for her and didn't see her sleeping in the corner. Was she waiting somewhere else for her? She could feel her heart beating hard against her chest and her eyes were smarting trying to hold back her tears as she ran quickly after the man. They went down long corridors to a kind of dormitory with two rows of narrow beds lined against the walls. Clean beds with real blankets, Sarah couldn't help noticing. A woman who seemed to be in charge said something to her in English which she didn't understand.

"What you saying? I don't understand. I don't spik English," she said desperately.

There was a brief discussion and a second woman approached.

"I speak Yiddish," she said. "I have to inform you that the relative who is your sponsor hasn't come for you. You'll have to…"

"Sponsor?" Sarah interrupted. She could feel a knot of panic in the pit of her stomach. "What is Sponsor? I don't understand what you're saying."

"A sponsor," the woman explained, "is a person, usually a relative, who has officially agreed to be responsible for you, give you a home and look after you. I was trying to tell you that your sponsor hasn't come for you. You must stay here tonight. Do you understand what I said?"

Sarah nodded, too choked up to speak.

"Don't worry," the woman said gently, looking at Sarah's

white face blotched with tears. "I guess she'll be here tomorrow. Here's a towel and some soap. Go and have a good wash. It will make you feel better. The washroom's through that door. We serve supper in half an hour."

Sarah walked to the washroom as if she was sleepwalking. "Aunt Manya hasn't come for me." These few words seem to pierce her brain and lock themselves in. "Aunt Manya hasn't come for me," she said to herself over and over again while at the same time trying hard to stop her tears. "Stop it! Stop it!" she hissed. "Pull yourself together Sarah Nossovsky, right now!" A good wash made her feel refreshed and she was hungry enough to eat anything. The first mouthful was a sure sign that the food was much better than anything she had eaten on the boat.

"Are you feeling better?" a young woman asked her. "We're all in the same boat here, you know," she sighed, pointing to a group of women chatting quietly together.

"Are you waiting for someone?" Sarah asked.

"The man I'm supposed to marry sent me a ticket but he didn't show up. They won't let me through without a sponsor. If he doesn't come within five days, I'll be deported."

"Five days? Deported? What d'you mean?"

"A new immigrant is allowed five days to wait here for his or her official sponsor to show up. Deported is the official word for being sent back home. That's the law," she said bitterly. "What are you doing here, child?"

"I'm waiting for my Aunt Manya. She didn't come today."

"She may have got the date wrong. It does happen. Don't give up hope, child. It'll all turn out for the best, you'll see. Have a good sleep. You look as if you need it."

Sarah spent a restless night tossing and turning and heard herself muttering, 'Five days!' over and over again until she woke with a throbbing head.

71

"Oh God," she moaned, holding her aching head. "If Aunt Manya doesn't come within five days I'll be deported back to HER." An icy feeling trickled down her spine. "I'm not going back. I don't care what happens to me but I'm never going back," she muttered through clenched teeth. Then she remembered the sad young woman's words: 'Don't ever give up hope.' If Aunt Manya has made a mistake about the date, she'll turn up here today, full of apologies. "I'm sure she will – won't you Aunt Manya?"

Where are you, Aunt Manya? You didn't come to Ellis Island today. Did you make a mistake with the dates? Mama, God rest her soul, used to say that every single person on earth makes a mistake or two sometime in his or her life. It's true isn't it? A lady who works here in Ellis Island is looking after me and gave me supper and a clean bed to sleep in last night. The funny thing is that all the time I was on the boat I thought of you waiting for me. Now it's my turn to be waiting for you. I do hope you'll come soon.

Chapter 11

The waiting room was cold and cheerless. The windows were too high up to see out of. "Who cares whether there's a view or not?" Sarah asked herself. "It's far more important to see who comes in." Whenever the door opened everyone stopped what they were doing, as if frozen in time, looking to see if their sponsors had arrived. If not they looked away quickly trying to find something to occupy the long empty hours of waiting. Sarah wiped the dust off her boots, untied her plaits and plaited them up again, packed and repacked her new canvas bag, and looked at the list of addresses Perle had written down for her. She tried to learn a few new English words in the notebook from Mrs Jensen but she found it hard to concentrate for long. "If only I knew why she hasn't come," she murmured sadly. "It wouldn't be as bad as thinking up any more excuses." The kind young woman's words came to her again. 'Don't ever give up hope.' She kept repeating them to herself as she sat quietly watching and waiting, her eyes fixed on the door. Little by little, as the day wore on, she heard a mocking voice from somewhere inside her head:

'Sarah Nossovsky,' it said, 'you are such a fool if you think Aunt Manya is coming now. Isn't it clear enough what's happened? She's changed her mind. She doesn't want you. You'll be deported, you'll be sent back home.' Her eyes were red and puffy from crying and the letters on her name tag were smudged with tears. She began to rummage at the bottom of her bag for some rag to wipe her nose when her fingers grasped her father's prayer book.

"Aunt Manya sent me Papa's prayer book and now it's come all the way back to New York! I wonder if it's a sign that she hasn't forgotten me," she murmured, stroking the book gently and putting it back in her bag.

Suddenly the door was opened by a man in a dark coat decorated with gold braid and brass buttons.

"Sarah Nossovsky." he called out.

Sarah leaped to her feet. She could feel her heart racing.

"Yes, me. I Sarah Nossovsky," she answered in a strange croaky voice which didn't sound like hers at all.

"Come this way."

He took her to a small room and pointed to a chair.

"Sit down. Wait here," he said and left her without another word.

She didn't have long to wait when two women walked in. Her heart seemed to miss a beat. *They both have very friendly faces,* she thought, *so one of them must be Aunt Manya! But which one? Which one?* Her eyes darted rapidly from one to the other.

The shorter woman had soft blue eyes and fair hair scraped back in a bun. The taller one was darker with a round face and a big smile.

"Please tell me which one of you is Aunt Manya?" she asked breathlessly.

The two women exchanged a quick glance and a nod, then the fair haired woman spoke.

"My name is Lena," she said quietly.

Sarah was half out of her seat ready to fling herself into the arms of the dark smiling woman when she heard her say, "And I'm Eva, Lena's sister."

Sarah dropped back into her seat and stared at them in disbelief. She felt the blood draining from her face and her legs suddenly felt as heavy as lead.

"You're not Aunt Manya?" She kept looking at them in case there had been some terrible mistake. "You're not Aunt Manya," she repeated. "Where is she? Why didn't she come? Doesn't she want me? Has she sent you to tell me she doesn't want me, has she?" she asked through her tears. "Well, has she?" she cried.

"My dear child," Eva sighed, taking Sarah's hand and gently stroking it. "We came to tell you that your Aunt Manya died last week. She had a heart attack. It was all very sudden."

Sarah sat staring in front of her. Then she buried her head in her hands as the terrible news sank in. "Aunt Manya is dead," she kept whispering to herself. At last she looked up, her face pale and strained. "First Papa and now Aunt Manya. She was my only family and now she's gone. I've nobody left. What am I going to do now? I wish I were dead too," she burst out, her whole body shaking with her sobs.

Together Lena and Eva folded Sarah into their arms and waited patiently until she had stopped crying. "Enough already," Eva said kindly, lifting her face towards her. "Your Aunt Manya wouldn't want all this, would she Lena?"

Lena shook her head and handed Sarah a handkerchief. "Here, dry your tears and listen to us. We may not be members of your family but we know you very well."

Sarah wiped her nose and looked up in surprise. "You do?"

"Yes we do. We saw a lot of your dear father, God rest his soul, when he was over here. He and Manya were always chatting together and if my memory serves me well," Lena said with a smile, "Sarah Nossovsky was always at the top of their list! Manya kept telling us what a brave little girl you were travelling all this way."

"Manya was our close friend," Eva added thoughtfully. "Lena and I came to ask you if you'd like to come and live with us. We've got the sponsor papers. It's all official. Will you?"

Sarah tried hard to say something, but the words wouldn't come. She just kept nodding her head until she found her voice again. At last she managed to say quickly all in the same breath:

"Yes, I want to come and live with you, I really do."

"Good," Eva nodded. "Lena and I were hoping you would. I guess we're the next best thing to family. I'm sure we'll all get along just fine, don't you think?" Eva asked.

Sarah nodded again. "It'll make it very special for me to live with Aunt Manya's two best friends."

"And for us too," Lena said. Then she pointed to the label the Immigration Officer had tied round Sarah's neck and said with a smile, "You're not going to need that anymore are you? After all, we know who you are!"

Sarah took off her name tag very slowly and looked down at the tear-stained name, 'Sarah Nossovsky.' "I'm going to keep this to remind me of my long journey. I almost threw it away when I thought that nobody was going to come for me. Then I changed my mind. I'm so glad I did because of all the thousands of immigrants in Ellis Island we might never have met without it, would we? So it really was meant to happen. It's beshert isn't it?" she asked.

"God bless you child," Eva and Lena murmured, "that's exactly what your Aunt Manya would have said. It's beshert."